this
little  ORCHARD
book belongs to

....

....

ORCHARD BOOKS
96 Leonard Street, London EC2A 4RH
Orchard Books Australia
14 Mars Road, Lane Cove, NSW 2066
1 86039 674 7 (hardback)
1 86039 810 3 (paperback)
First published in Great Britain in 1998
Printed in Italy

Freddie goes swimming

Nicola Smee

little 🍀 ORCHARD

I'd like to be able to
swim like my fish.
So would Bear.

Mum takes us to the
swimming pool.

Not the big pool, the little learner's pool.

I'm ready!

But Bear's not.
He doesn't want
to get wet.

The water's lovely
when you're in!

Mum says I won't swallow
the water if I keep my
mouth closed ...

...but it goes up my nose as well!

"You'll soon learn, Freddie"
says Mum.

So I practise ...

and practise.

Until at last ...

I can swim just like my fish!